SHREDDERMAN

SECRET IDENTITY

bY: WENdELiN VAn DrAAnEN

iLLUSTrATED bY: BriAN BiggS

SCHOLASTIC INC.
New York Toronto London Auckland Sydney
Mexico City New Delhi Hong Kong Buenos Aires

ISBN-13: 978-0-439-89755-6

ISBN-10: 0-439-89755-6

Text copyright © 2004 by Wendelin Van Draanen Parsons.
Illustrations copyright © 2004 by Brian Biggs. All rights reserved.
Published by Scholastic Inc., 557 Broadway, New York, NY 10012,
by arrangement with Random House Children's Books, a division of
Random House, Inc. SCHOLASTIC and associated logos are
trademarks and/or registered trademarks of Scholastic Inc.

12 11 10   11/0

Printed in the U.S.A.   40

First Scholastic printing, September 2006

WEndELiN Van DrAAnEN

For Colton, my inspiration.

BriAN Bigg$S

*A truckload of thanks to Wilson,
Elliot, and Jessica for keeping an
eye on each other and remembering
to take me out to play.
A special thank you goes to Isabel and
Nancy for taking the chance.*

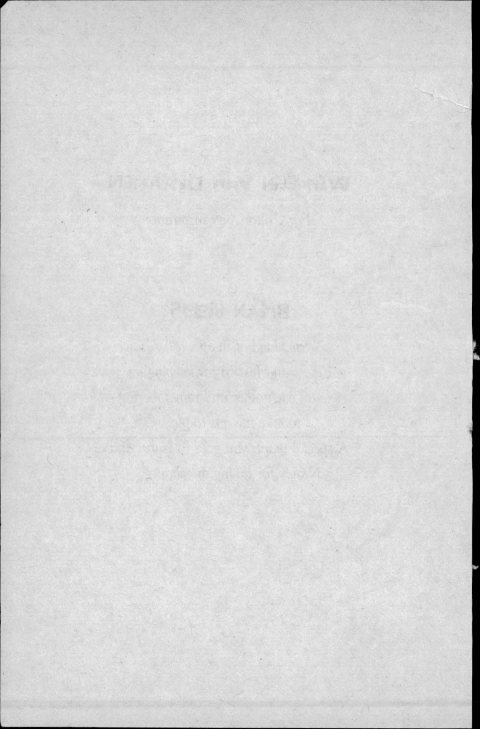

CONTENTS

CHAPTER 1
Bubba Bixby

Bubba Bixby was born big and mean, full of teeth and ready to bite.

That's what my mom thinks anyway.

My dad says a boy isn't born bad—he grows into being bad.

I don't know who's right. What I *do* know is that Bubba Bixby's got rocky knuckles.

And killer breath.

Teachers are always telling him to use words instead of fists—they have no idea what they're saying! Bubba-breath can knock you out cold.

Ask Ian McCoy. It actually happened to him in the third grade. When Bubba shouted at him, Ian's eyes rolled up in his head.

His knees buckled.

Then he blacked out and bit the dirt.

We had to slap his cheeks like crazy to get him to wake up, and when he did, he sat up, then *threw* up.

My father thinks I shouldn't call Bubba "Bubba" like everyone else does. He thinks I should call him Alvin, which is his real name. I've told him that calling him Alvin will get me pounded. Mike McDermish got dared to do it once and was nothing but Mike-mush when it was over. Now it's "Sure, Bubba" and "You betcha, Bubba" whenever he talks to him.

My mom and dad used to try to get the school to do something about Bubba. They talked to teachers. They even talked to the principal, Dr. Voss, a bunch of times. Nothing changed.

Dad thinks Dr. Voss isn't assertive enough. Dr. Voss thinks *I'm* not assertive enough. She says that kids like Bubba help us get ready for life.

Now that I'm a fifth grader, my dad tells me

not to worry about Bubba. He says that I've got a lot more on the ball than Bubba does, and that one day Alvin Bixby will be working for me.

But he's wrong on two counts. First, that's forever away. And second, I wouldn't hire Bubba in a million years.

I'd fire him.

Say...what if I could fire Bubba from school? Wouldn't that be cool? Just kick him out and tell him to never come back. I could eat lunch without him flipping over my tray. Play four-square without him hogging the ball. Line up for class without him taking cuts and shoving the rest of us back. Oh, yeah. School without Bubba would be a whole new place.

I have to admit that our teacher, Mr. Green, *tries* to keep Bubba in line, but Mr. Green's already got one full-time job teaching fifth grade, and my mom says it's hard for him to take on another in the middle of it.

Plus, Bubba's sly. So no matter how hard Mr. Green tries, Bubba gets away with stuff.

Like lying.

And cheating.

And stealing.

My magic-rub eraser is in Bubba's desk right now with the initials B.B. gouged into it. So are some of my colored pencils. And probably my favorite *The Gecko and Sticky* magazine and the *Dinosaurs* library book I keep getting a reminder on.

It's not just my stuff that gets stolen. Bubba

takes things from everybody. Even his friends, Kevin and Max. Actually, I think he steals from them the most.

The only thing Bubba's ever *given* anyone is names. I used to be Nolan Byrd. Now I'm Byrd-the-Nerd.

Or just plain Nerd.

Jake is Bucktooth. Trey is Butthead. Marvin is Moron. Todd is Toad, Ian is Fizz, Jenni is Worm lips, Trinity is Pony-girl, Kayla is Freckle, Sarah is Kiss-up...everyone's got two names:

one from their parents and one from Bubba.

His names stick, too. If Bubba calls you something a few times, you'll hear it over and over again from everyone. Some people *like* their names. Like Brian Washington. Even the teachers call him Gap because he wants them to. He doesn't *have* a gap between his front teeth anymore, but Bubba called him that in second grade, and he hasn't been Brian since.

So that's Bubba. He calls you names. He steals your stuff. He breathes putrid fumes in your face.

And even though I've always wanted to *do* something about it, I could never figure out what. I'm half Bubba's size and don't exactly want to *die* in elementary school.

So I just eat lunch far away from him, make room when he's cutting in line, and let him call me Nerd.

It's not fair, but at least I'm still alive.

CHAPTER 2
Mr. Green, Homework Machine

Mr. Green likes animals.

And plants.

And rocks and sand and *skulls*.

One side of our classroom is set up like the desert. The other is like a jungle. The jungle has a waterfall that he turns on when we're taking tests. It's supposed to relax us and help us think, but all it does is make me have to use the bathroom.

Some kids—like Bubba—think Mr. Green's weird, but I think he's cool. Bubba calls him the Happy Hippie because he's got a ponytail, he likes to play guitar, and he wears jeans and sandals to school. He also drives an old van with dolphins painted all over it that everyone calls the Green Machine.

Every month, Mr. Green gives us a project to do. A *hard* project. We've had to build all kinds of things:

Ecosystems.

Solar systems.

Igloos.

The Great Pyramids!

And since my mom and dad think it's good exercise for me to do my own work, my projects are always disasters.

My igloo looked half melted.

My pyramids crumbled on the way to school.

The trees in my ecosystem looked like pencils with hula grass.

My solar system looked like it really had gone through the Big Bang.

Give me ten pages of triple-digit multiplication. Twenty! But don't ask me to build pyramids

or create the universe. I'm still working on tying my shoes so they don't come undone in P.E.

So when Mr. Green strummed his guitar and announced, "Listen up, gang. Time to tune in to this month's project," I groaned and flopped my head on my desk.

Mr. Green looked at me with a smile. "You're gonna dig this one, Nolan. I promise."

My head stayed put. If it was a project, I was going to hate it.

"This month you get to design your own newspaper page," he said. "Your mission is to go around Cedar Valley and bring back our friends Who, What, When, Where, and Why. You can choose any topic you want. All I'm asking is that you follow these guidelines!" He wagged a stack of lime green papers and said, "Don't lose this sheet! It lists everything you need for an A." He started passing them out to the different tables, which are just four desks pushed together. "If you can check off everything on this list, you'll get an A, guaranteed! And please note the last item." He pointed and read, "*Turn this sheet in with your project.*" He went back to passing them out. "I will not—hear me now, gang—I will *not* give you replacements if you lose yours."

He counted out four sheets at our table and handed them to Randy Ricardo, next to me.

Randy handed one to me, one to Trinity, and one to Freddy, across from him.

Then Mr. Green said, "And yes, you read that right. You *may* use your computer on this one."

I sat up a little. What was that? He always made us do *every*thing by hand.

"If you have software at home that's designed for page layout and you know how to use it, use it!"

I sat straight up.

My jaw dropped.

Was I dreaming?

"Or you can use your word-processing skills, then print and paste. Book some time with Miss Surkit in the computer lab. She's expecting you! *Or* if you want to do the whole thing by hand, that's cool with me." He shook the last table's papers in the air and said, "However you decide to do it, follow this sheet!"

He went back to his director's chair, saying, "And yes, you *may* use clip art. You *may* scan in photos. You *may* use a digital camera, if you've got one. Or if you're not a fan of computers, you may draw your illustrations."

I blinked like crazy.

I shook out one ear.

I could use my digital camera?

For *homework?*

He looked my way and grinned. "Some of you are thinkin', Outtasight! Some of you are thinkin', Aw, maaaaan—but all of you will grow from the experience, so remember…" He picked up his guitar again, strummed through some familiar chords, and right on cue we all sang out, "Attitude is everything!"

He swung the guitar back onto its stand. "Right on! Now let's dig into the details. We've got until the bell rings to hammer this thing out."

The more he went over the green sheet, the more excited I got.

No glue!

No crackers or plaster or feathers!

No poster board or craft paper or scissors!

I'd be able to work at the computer for *hours* every day without Mom and Dad telling me to shut down. I'd get to use the scanner and the camera and the Internet . . . this was going to be great!

When Mr. Green was done going over the project sheet, he asked us to put our heads down. "Close your eyes. Meditate. What do *you* want to report on? You could do your project on someone in Cedar Valley," he said. "It could be a historical piece about Old Town. You could write about the animal shelter. Report on the new hospital they're building across the river. Profile a local sports hero.

"The most important thing is, pick a subject that interests you. It will be much easier for you to write about something you like.

"Or . . . hate. Consider that! Is there something that you feel very angry about? An injustice you see in the world? That would be fine, too. *Anything* will be fine so long as you follow the green sheet."

I was too excited to close my eyes. So while the kids around me were dreaming up their stories—or just falling asleep—my eyes were cranked wide open. I didn't care *what* I wrote about. I cared about the gear!

I'd use everything!

Then at Table 6, I noticed something. Bubba's hand was reaching over to Miriam Wipple's desk. He was peeking through slits in his eyes.

What was he doing?

I jammed my lids shut. Then I cracked them open, just enough to watch.

Bubba was smooth.

Real smooth.

And before any-

one noticed, he had Miriam's green sheet in his hand.

In his lap.

In his folder.

Two things stopped me from telling on him: One, school was over in seventeen seconds. Bubba'd be out the door before I could get to Mr. Green. And two, I was tingling from ear to toe. I had an idea that would make Bubba Bixby sorry he'd ever called us names.

Or swiped our stuff.

Or breathed his trashy breath down our throats.

I'd do my report on an injustice, all right.

I'd do my report on Bubba Bixby!

CHAPTER 3
Spy Tools

I raced home and almost ripped the screen door getting inside. "Mom! You'll never guess what!"

"Well, hi, honey," she said from her desk. "What?"

"I get to use my computer! I don't have to write anything longhand! Or cut or glue or *break* anything!"

She laughed. "For...?"

"This month's project! I can use my scanner and my digital camera! I can use anything!"

"Really?"

I threw my backpack down and yanked out the green sheet. "See?"

She skimmed the paper.

"So don't kick me off my computer, okay? It's homework!"

"Hmmm," she said, handing it back. "No tears over this one, huh? Plus, you're lucky because your father will probably love helping you out."

Uh-oh. She was right. My dad's a reporter for the *Cedar Valley Gazette*, so this project was right up his alley. But I didn't want him to know what I was planning! There was no way he'd let me do my project on Bubba Bixby!

"So how'd the rest of your day go?" Mom asked. "Alvin give you trouble?"

"Huh?" I was still thinking about how to *not* tell my dad about the project. "Oh. Just the usual."

"Do you want to tell me about it?"

"Nah. Everything's fine." I tried to sound casual. Tried to sound cool. And after my snack, I hurried to my room and closed the door tight. It was my turn to give Bubba Bixby a little trouble!

First step—digital camera. I was going to catch him in the act!

Second step—jacket. I needed someplace to hide the camera so no one would see I was taking pictures.

I tore through my closet.

I pulled out two jackets.

I tried every pocket.

None of them would work.

What about my backpack?

I emptied it.

I tried all the compartments.

The little one was a good size, but using my backpack would put the camera *behind* me. How could I take pictures like that?

Wait! The camera had a remote control! It was small, too. I could hide it in my hand, easy!

I dug through my desk until I found it. I put the camera in remote mode and tried it out.

It worked great!

I put the camera behind me, like it would be in my backpack. I tried the remote from all kinds of angles until I got my moves down. All I had to do was reach around a little. Or put my fist on my hip. Or cross my arms like I was mad. The remote worked great!

I checked out my backpack. I needed to make some kind of opening for the camera lens and remote sensor. Some kind of window to take pictures through.

But I couldn't just cut a hole. Everyone would see the camera! I needed some kind of flap in front of the lens that I could open and close.

And when the flap was open, there needed to be some kind of screen that would camouflage the lens without blocking it. Something that would let the camera see *out* without letting people see *in*.

How was I going to do *that*?

Then I had an idea.

But it was going to mean using scissors.

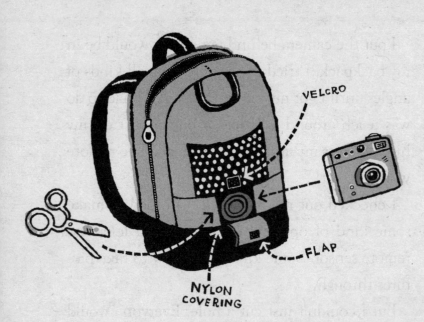

VELCRO

FLAP

NYLON
COVERING

And worse, a needle and thread.

Did I really want to do this? Did I really want to jab myself a hundred times with a needle? Did I really want to cut up my backpack? This was a *great* backpack.

My mind flashed on a picture of Bubba breathing down my throat like he had so many times.

Of him calling me Nerd.

Of him stealing stuff.

Oh, yeah. It was worth it.

I charged down the hall and tore through my mother's sewing kit.

Needle—check!

Thread—check!

Velcro—yes! She had Velcro!

Then I dug through her scraps box and...yes! There was an old black nylon that would work great as a screen!

"Nolan?" my mom called down the hall. "What are you doing?"

"Nothing, Mom!"

I crammed the nylon in my pocket.

I shoved her sewing kit back in the closet.

I tried to hide the spool of thread and Velcro in my fists but jabbed myself with the needle.

Blood squirted from my palm.

I clamped my mouth over it.

"Nothing?" Mom asked, coming at me.

Closer.

And closer!

"Nuh-uh," I said, lapping up blood. "Well, I, uh, I have to sew something."

"*Sew* something?"

"Uh-huh." I edged around her. Past her.

"Sew what? You want me to do it for you?"

"No!"

She was giving me her suspicious look.

"It's personal, okay?" I charged back to my room, closed the door tight, and waited for her to knock.

Knock-knock-knock.

I cracked the door open. "I need some privacy, okay?"

"Privacy?" She seemed hurt.

"Please, Mom...?"

"Hmmm. Well, Mr. Privacy, I just came down to tell you that *The Gecko and Sticky* is on."

"It is?"

"Uh-huh."

"Can you . . . can you tape it?"

"No!"

"Well, it's probably a rerun anyway." I started to close the door.

"Nolan!" She pushed back a little. "What *are* you up to that you're willing to miss *The Gecko and Sticky?*"

"Mom, please. I just need some privacy, okay?"

"Am I going to be mad when I find out what you're doing?"

"No! I promise, you won't."

She just stood there.

I just stood there.

Finally she sighed and said, "Okay."

I worked and worked until dinnertime, when my mom made me take a break. And when she told Dad about my new project, sure enough, he got all excited.

"I can help you with this! I can get you access to practically anyone in town. How about the mayor? You want to interview him? Think of how impressed Mr. Green would be!"

"Uh, I don't think I want to interview the mayor, Dad."

"Oh. Well, who do you have in mind, Nolan?"

"Uh...I'm not sure...."

"How about Mr. Zilch?"

"Your boss?" I asked. "Why would I want to interview him? I thought you didn't like him."

Mom looked at Dad.

Dad looked at Mom.

Finally Dad said, "I never said I didn't like Mr. Zilch...."

"Well, *do* you?"

"How about Sergeant Klubb?" Mom hurried to ask. "It would be real interesting to interview a policeman, don't you think?"

"Say...that would be a great choice," my dad said. "Sarge is a very nice man. He'd probably let you cruise around Cedar Valley in his squad car."

"Um...let me think about it, okay?" I downed the rest of my milk and picked up my plate. "May I be excused?"

"To get back to work on your project?" Mom asked.

I nodded.

"But, Nolan, if you haven't even picked out

who to interview, how can you be working on your project?"

"Uh . . . I'm getting the gear together, Mom."

"The gear?"

I nodded. "May I be excused?"

She sighed.

I took that as a yes, bussed my dishes, and hurried down to my room.

The mayor—ha!

Mr. Zilch—ha!

Sergeant Klubb—ha!

Interviews with them wouldn't compare to the piece I was going to do on Bubba Bixby!

I got back to work, and by bedtime my backpack was converted. My fingers were sore and bloody, but I'd done it! My backpack had a little fold-down flap for the camera lens. It had a backup layer of black nylon to camouflage it. The sides and bottom were padded with a cut-up T-shirt.

And the cool thing is, it worked.

I'd made a spy-pack, and it actually worked!

The next morning, I got up early and practiced taking pictures backward.

I had to be sly.

I had to be smooth.

I had to act like I'm not used to acting.

At breakfast Mom said, "Forget your hair, Nolan?"

My hair has a life of its own. I felt around my head. It was sticking out on one side again. "Sorry."

"And, Nolan? Your socks go *inside* your pants, remember?" my dad said.

I looked down. How had that happened? Again? I pulled my pant leg out of my sock. "Whoops."

"Try putting your socks on first, champ. Works for me," my dad said.

"I know. I know."

My mom kissed me on the forehead. "We're just trying to help you outgrow your nickname, honey."

I looked at her. Then at my dad. "You mean Nerd?"

Dad nodded. "There's a lot you could do to *not* have people call you that, you know."

"Like combing your hair," Mom said gently.

"And keeping your shoes tied," Dad said.

"And matching your clothes." My mom looked me over. "Isn't that the T-shirt you slept in?"

"Huh? I ... I don't remember." I really didn't.

"Preoccupied with something again?" my father asked.

"Yeah, honey. You've got bags," my mom said, zooming in on my eyes. "Did you sleep all right?"

I shoved some peanut-buttered Eggo into my mouth. "I was thinking about my project."

"Ah," my dad said. "So have you decided who you'd like to interview?"

"Uh ... not yet."

"I hope you don't think I was being too pushy last night. I was just excited to be able to help."

"I know, Dad."

"Well, let me know when you decide, okay?" He pointed a fork at my plate. "Uh ... don't you want syrup on that?"

"Nuh-uh," I said, shoveling the rest of the Eggo

in my mouth. No time for syrup—I had to get going.

I had spy tools to try out.

Bullies to catch!

Starting today, Bubba Bixby would have to watch out for *me*.

CHAPTER 4
Level 42-e

I was afraid to run with my backpack on. The camera was in nice and tight, but I was still worried I'd jolt it loose. So I did what Mom calls my power-walk. I use it all the time when teachers or lifeguards are yelling, "Don't run!"

It gets you places fast.

People make fun of my power-walk, so I only use it when I really, really, *really* want to get somewhere quick. And school was someplace I wanted to get to quick!

A couple of older kids called, "Hey, Nerd! Slow down," as I trucked onto the playground. I just ignored them, though. I don't think they even know me.

Bubba was nowhere. I checked the upper field. The lower field.

I checked the four-square courts and the basketball courts.

I looked behind and even between all the "portables," which are the classrooms that look like flat-roofed mobile homes, only they never go anywhere.

I even checked in all the boys' bathrooms, just in case.

Mr. Hoover, the janitor, must have noticed me running around because he grinned and asked, "Lose another sweatshirt, Nolan?"

"Uh, no, sir," I said. "Just looking for someone."

"Ah," he said, and walked away, still grinning.

Then I spotted Bubba, cutting across the lower field, with Kevin on one side and Max on the other. They were laughing about something, and for some reason it made me mad. How come a bully like Bubba had friends and I didn't?

The last bell rang, so I went into our classroom. I didn't want any of the other kids to think there was something strange about my backpack, so I hid it under my desk. I took out my pencil box and homework folder, my dictionary and all my books.

Randy shook his head and said, "Why *do* you take all that stuff home every day, Nerd?"

I looked right at him. "So nobody steals it."

"Steals it? Who's gonna steal that stuff? You

think *I'm* gonna steal it? You couldn't *pay* me to steal that stuff, Nerd."

Trinity Althoffer whispered, "Don't be so mean, Randy."

Randy shrugged. "I'm not being mean. Am I, Nerd?"

He wasn't really. Not compared to some kids. But in my head, something happened. Something snapped. "Well, you're not exactly being *nice*," I told him. "And would you mind? My name's Nolan."

His eyes got sort of big. "Yeah? Then why's everyone call you Nerd?"

"Same reason people call you Ricardo-Retardo. Same reason people call her Pony-girl and him Pee-boy." I looked from Trinity to Freddy to Randy. "I don't call any of you those names, so stop calling me Nerd."

Randy looked across the table at Freddy, then back at me. "Whatever you say...Nerd!"

He and Freddy busted up.

Trinity went back to coloring the pony on her folder.

I got madder than ever.

I didn't let *them* know that. I kept my anger inside. But instead of staying in my throat like it usually does, it started burning through me. All around inside me. I felt hot. And sharp. Like I would zap people if I touched them.

I snuck out a finger and touched Randy's sleeve.

Nothing happened.

During the flag salute, I watched Bubba out of the corner of my eye.

He had scissors.

Miriam had hair.

I knew what he was thinking.

I reached down for my backpack. I tried to be smooth. Sly. Cool. I could catch him digitally! I could *nail* him.

Instead, I stepped on my shoelace and crashed

to the ground during "...with liberty and justice for all."

My chair went flying.

Miriam's hair had a chunk missing.

So did my rear end, where I'd clipped the chair. At least that's what it felt like. It hurt *bad*.

"You okay?" Mr. Green asked.

"Yeah. Fine," I lied, sliding back into my chair. "Sorry."

"That's all right." He watched me a second, then called for absences. When that was done, he held up a stack of papers and said, "Fractions time-trials are graded, gang. Some of you have work to do. Some of you," he looked my way, "ought to be in high school."

Randy said, "Nerd," under his breath.

I almost said, "Retardo!" back, but I didn't.

Mr. Green started handing out papers, saying, "You need a seventy-*five* to go to the next level, gang. Seventy doesn't cut it anymore."

He gave back the papers at our table, and before anyone could see mine, I folded it in half.

Trinity got seventy-five on level 7-a. That's where most kids were. Somewhere on level 7. Randy folded his, too, but I saw the score. Fifty on level 5-d. Freddy said, "Hey! I passed!" and showed everyone his eighty. Level 8-b. Then he looked at me and said, "Get another perfect, Nerd?"

"My name's Nolan," I said quietly.

He ignored me. "What level are you on, anyway?"

I ignored *him*. But I was dying to know what my score was, so I peeked inside.

One hundred percent.

Level 42-e.

Oh, yeah.

"You did, didn't you, Nerd," Freddy said. "I can tell by that stupid look on your face. What level? Twelve?"

"He's in the forties, Freddy," Trinity said. "And leave him alone."

"Forties? There's no such thing!"

"Leave him *alone*," she said again.

Freddy took another look at his eighty and stuffed it in his desk.

I smiled a little at Trinity.

She smiled a little back.

Then I opened my paper again. Mr. Green had written something on the bottom of it, and I wanted to see what it was.

I smiled big when I saw it: *Nolan—You shred, man! Awesome!*

I shred?! Shred was special. Beyond awesome. He only said that about his favorite guitar players.

Or bands.

Or *presidents*.

I put the paper carefully in my folder.

Inside I could feel it—
things were changing.

CHAPTER 5
Secret Identity

By the end of the day, Miriam's hair was missing a chunk, Slow Jim, the class tortoise, had a new design on his shell, and Ian and Danielle's green sheets had disappeared.

I thought I'd gotten a picture of Slow Jim's run-in with the Magic Markers. I really did. But at recess when I hid in a bathroom stall and checked out the shot, all I saw was Bubba's butt. It took up the whole frame.

I was too slow with Ian and Danielle, too. Their green sheets were gone before I could get ready.

So I got no good shots the first day. But I didn't give up. I started taking my backpack everywhere with me because one, I didn't want anything to happen to my camera, and two, I didn't want to miss catching Bubba red-handed.

Kids called me a nerd, but for once I didn't care. Not that much, anyway.

I was on assignment.

I was on a mission.

Bubba started it, I was going to finish it.

All week during lunch recess I didn't play four-square. I wore my backpack and tried to get better at taking pictures with my back turned. I wrote down what I was doing in a little notebook. Every shot. Then I went into a bathroom stall with my backpack and scanned through the pictures. Sometimes the remote hadn't worked. Sometimes I was off by a mile. My notes would say, *Miriam at fountain*, and my shot would be half of somebody I didn't even know.

Then on Friday I caught him. On camera. In the act of dumping one of the trash cans. Looking over his shoulder. Can in the air. Trash flying out.

It was the perfect shot.

I stayed in the stall ten minutes just looking at it.

After school I got to work. I loaded the picture into my computer, tweaked the color, cut the frame. It was beautiful.

And now...what? I had to write an article. Actually, according to the green sheet, I had to write a lot of articles. One of which was supposed to be an interview.

Uh-oh.

And now that I had my picture, I didn't really know what I wanted to *do* with it. What was going to happen to me anyway, once I turned my project in? Mr. Green always displayed projects.

Everyone would see!

Which was what I'd wanted, only now I was scared. When Bubba saw it, he'd pound me!

The more I thought about it, the more stupid doing a project on Bubba Bixby seemed. If only there was a way for everyone to see it, but not have anyone know who'd done it.

But how was I going to do that?

I took a break to watch *The Gecko and Sticky*. It was another rerun, but one of my favorite episodes. In it, Chase Morton—who is *The* Gecko—and Sticky—who is *a* gecko—save their town from the clutches of Damien Black. It's one of my

favorites because in the end Damien falls—
aaaaaaaarrrrrr—into a pit of tarantulas. You
should see him freak out and call, "Mommy!
Mommy!" It's hilarious.

But after the show was over, I went back to
thinking about my project. How was I ever going
to do it without Bubba knowing it was me?

Maybe I should just change subjects. Dad and
Mom still asked me about my project, but not as
much. And I knew that Dad was sort of upset that
I didn't want his help. Maybe I should just forget
about Bubba. I'd lived with him this long, I could
survive a couple more years, right?

But something about the past few days had
made me feel...strong. Like I was finally *doing*
something about being pushed around. But I
didn't know where to go from here. Forward was
scary, but back seemed worse.

I decided to do an extra credit math puzzle Mr.
Green had passed out. They were always fun! But

as I was going through my binder, I saw my fractions time-trial. Level 42-e. One hundred percent. *Nolan—You shred, man!*

Maybe everyone else thought I was a nerd, but Mr. Green didn't. He thought I shred! It was like he could see the Nolan that was hidden by the Nerd.

And that's when I got the idea.

Maybe I could have a secret identity!

Like Chase Morton was The Gecko!

And Clark Kent was Superman!

And Peter Parker was Spider-Man.

Maybe I could become someone else!

Someone better than the Nerd! Inside, I had lots of ideas that were cool and funny. Inside, I was strong and quick and didn't trip on my shoelaces. Inside, I had room for lots of friends.

I leaned back in my chair and closed my eyes. I pictured myself in a superhero's costume. I thought about what superpowers I could have.

Maybe I'd have an eye that was really a camera lens.

Cool!

Maybe I'd have telekinetic powers and could move stuff around.

Double cool!

Or maybe I could fly. I've always thought that would be the absolute coolest!

I opened my eyes and sat up. Flying. *Sheez.* The only flying I'd ever done was off a swing, and I almost broke my arm landing. That, and one time when I animated a picture of myself so it flew across my computer screen.

Thinking about that made something in my brain go *snap.* And for a minute I just sat there with my eyes wide open, frozen in place.

Then I jumped straight out of my chair.

Maybe I couldn't fly around the playground or the classroom. But I *could* fly. And I *could* have a secret identity.

On the Internet!

My mind was spinning like crazy. My legs were walking me all over the room! What if I built a Web site and posted my project on it!

I could totally shred on Bubba!

I could put up pictures! Stories! Jokes!
Evidence!

It would be All Bubba, All the Time.

Oh, yeah!

I logged on to my computer and started typing like crazy. I needed a domain name for my Web site. What was my secret identity going to be? Not *nerd.com*. No way. More like *shred.com*. Yeah! I went to a registration site to see if it was taken.

Drat! It was.

I tried *youshred.com*.

Available, but sorta lame.

The Shredder! How about that? It'd be like The Gecko!

I typed it in.

Taken.

Then all of a sudden I had it. Shredderman. Like a superhero, flying though cyberspace, fighting for truth and justice!

It was perfect!

I typed it in with my fingers crossed—not an easy thing to do! But then the screen flashed with... *this domain is still available.*

"Oh, yeah!" I jumped up and pumped the air with my fist. "Shredderman!"

I was on my way to becoming a cyber-superhero.

CHAPTER 6
Building the Site

No one can know a superhero's identity.

Not even his mother.

So I wound up *promising* her I wasn't doing anything bad, wound up *begging* her to trust me. Wound up on my knees, waving cash in the air, *praying* for her to give me her credit card number.

It costs money to put up a Web site, you know.

I also wound up cleaning my room. "How can I trust a boy with a messy room?" she asked me. I didn't see the connection, but I made it shipshape anyway.

Then came the refrigerator. Maybe she can't trust a boy with a messy refrigerator? Don't ask me. I just cleaned it. Also the kitchen sink. Then the driveway. Dad came home and they talked it over.

Dad shrugged a lot.

Mom shook her head plenty.

I couldn't hear a word of what they were saying.

After dinner I cleared the table. Loaded the dishes. Emptied the garbage. Trust was everywhere.

Finally Mom sat me down and said, "All right."

"Wa-hoo!"

"Only *I'm* going to type in the number."

"No, Mom! You can't. This is top-secret! It's…it's…vital to the operation that I do it myself."

"To the…operation? Nolan, what *are* you up to?"

"Mom, please! Write it down on a piece of paper. I'll give it right back. You can burn it! I'll never use it again. Promise!"

She just frowned at me.

"Have I ever done anything that you wouldn't want me to?"

She was quiet a minute, then said, "We're not talking about recycling paper in the bathroom sink, right? Or microwaving the ice cream carton for five minutes to make a milkshake? Or luring an ant invasion outside with a trail of sugar water?"

"No!"

"We're talking big things?"

"Right."

She thought some more. "Well, no... but you *are* approaching puberty."

"Mo-om! I'm in the fifth grade!"

Dad was in the room. He shrugged. Mom closed her eyes. Finally she sighed and said, "This is the one and only time I'm going to go for this. You'd better not let me down, Nolan."

"I won't, Mom! I promise I won't!"

"Okay, then."

Shredderman.com became mine that night.

WebBuilder came flying through cyberspace seconds later. Complete with E-Z Launch instructions.

I had the tools. I had the site. Time to start building!

But I'd barely had a chance to print out the instructions when Mom knocked on the door.

I shut off the computer monitor. "Come in!"

"Honey? It's past bedtime."

"But it's Friday!"

Her eyes narrowed. Her hands punched both sides of her waist.

"Oops. Sorry," I said. "I'm going."

I went, all right. But I couldn't sleep. All I could think about was being Shredderman. And besides, superheroes don't need sleep, right?

So when Mom and Dad went to bed, I waited until I was sure *they* were asleep, then I booted up and got building.

By morning my home page had an awesome look. Cool font. Radical colors. Across the top was:

Welcome to Shredderman.com, where truth and justice prevail!

Then a purple and gold SHREDDERMAN banner waved as a masked cartoon guy zoomed

from one corner of the screen to the other. That was the hard part, but it was so, so cool!

At six-thirty I heard the toilet flush. I saved quick, then shut down the computer, hid the instructions under my pillow, and hopped into bed.

The next thing I knew, Mom was shaking me, saying, "Nolan! Nolan, it's nearly noon, honey. You've got to get up!"

Noon? How could it be *noon*? I sat up. Had I dreamt the whole thing? My hand shot under my pillow. Nuh-uh. The instructions were right there.

"Are you all right?" she asked me. "You've got bags again."

"I . . . I couldn't get to sleep."

"Mmm," she said. "Well, it's definitely time to get up. Your dad's gone into work for a few hours, and I want to get some groceries." She patted my leg. "Come on, honey."

I dragged behind her in the store. I dragged some more carrying in the groceries. But the instant she told me I could go work on the computer, *zingo*, I woke right up. Time to shred!

I spent Saturday night up all night again. And Sunday I was worthless. Again. Sunday night I tried to forget about Shredderman and get some sleep. I couldn't be worthless at school! I had time-trials to ace. Pictures of Bubba to take. Lots more pictures of Bubba!

My computer was shut down but my brain wasn't. At eleven-fifteen I finally gave in and snuck out of bed. And by the time the toilet was flushing Monday morning, the site was really shaping up. I had a *Bubba Jokes* link that had stuff like:

Q: Why did the bully steal the trick-or-treater's candy bag?

A: He wanted some Bubba-gum!
and . . .

Q: What do you call a bully fire?

A: A Bubba-que!

and...

Q: Why run from a bully?

A: He's got the Bub-onic plague!

I had a **Bubba, Caught in the Act** link where I posted the picture of him dumping the trash can all over the ground.

And my favorite—a link called **Bubba's Big Butt**.

That's all it was, too. That picture I'd taken of Bubba's butt. Made me laugh every time I clicked the link.

I also had a link that said, *What's big and fat and smells all over? (Click here)* that took you straight back to that same picture.

It had been a great night.

I shut down quick and got packed for school.

Camera—check!

Memory card—check!

Recharged battery—check!

Remote control—check!

I even remembered to put my socks on first.

I wasn't tired—I was wired!

Wired, and ready to *shred*.

CHAPTER 7
Flip-o-rama

I was crossing the street to school when I had an idea. Why just pictures of Bubba? My camera had a movie-clip mode! It took up a lot of memory, but who cared? What if I could get movie clips of Bubba-boy in action? Stealing stuff. Shoving second graders. Throwing food.

Live-action reporting—oh, yeah!

Also, I had to start being more careful. If I didn't want anyone to know who Shredderman was, I couldn't shoot Bubba in the classroom anymore. If my shots came from inside Mr. Green's room, everyone would know it was someone in his class.

Pretty soon everyone would figure out it was me.

So I stopped using my camera in class. Instead, I planned new ways to shred on him.

I thought up a cartoon strip: *Alvin and the Dumbmunks*, starring Alvin "Bubba" Bixby and his chattering chipmunk chums, Kevin and Max. I'd get *Alvin and the Chipmunks* pictures off the Internet—there had to be some! Then I'd scan in Max and Kevin and Bubba from last year's yearbook, shrink their faces, and superimpose them on chipmunk bodies. Add a few bubble shapes for their words...I was cracking up just thinking about it!

But at recess, I stopped planning and got gutsy. I followed Bubba around. I hid between buildings. Behind bushes. I spent a lot of time pretending to tie my shoes.

I started listening to what other kids were saying about Bubba. I started listening to what he was saying to other kids. I took notes. I was a data-collection machine!

Then on Tuesday I got my interview:

Kevin: "What'cha doin' after school today, Bubba?"

Bubba: "Pickin' my nose, what d'ya think, stupid?"

Max: "Oh, yeah—I can't come over today, Bubba."

Bubba: "Why not?"

Max: "I... Mom says I have to work on my newspaper project."

Bubba: "Tell yo mama to do your project."

Kevin: "Yeah, man. Tell yo mama to do your project."

Bubba: "All you have to do is smile like this, see? Then sniff like this, see? Boo-hoo-hoo. It's easy. Get yo mama to do your work."

Max: "Does yours really do yours?"

Bubba: "You think *I'm* gonna do that Happy Hippie assignment? Get real."

Maybe it didn't have all of Who-What-When-Where-Why in it, but it wasn't bad! And I didn't have to ask him a single question.

Then on Wednesday it happened. I'd just sat down with my lunch. My backpack was next to me, on the table. The flap was open. My remote was ready. Bubba walked into the cafeteria. He saw the teachers were busy helping clean up a spill, and smiled. And I could tell from across the room—he was in the mood for a flip-o-rama.

He did it to some little kids.

He did it quick.

He put his fingers under the lip of a tray and *flip*. He tipped food all over a little kid. Then *flip, flip, flip, flip*—he went right down the row!

Chicken nuggets went flying!

Orange slices splatted on the floor!

Jell-O was wiggling everywhere!

And Bubba ditched it out the side door before the teachers had turned around.

I almost couldn't believe it. It had happened right in front of me! I was so excited I was shaking. I grabbed my backpack, left my lunch, and headed straight for the bathroom.

By the time I saw Bubba standing by the bath-room sinks, it was too late. Max and Kevin were with him, so I was surrounded.

I threw it in reverse and tried to run out the door, but Bubba grabbed me and said, "Hey, Nerd. You come in here too much, you know that?"

I kept my mouth shut. I didn't want him to hear me shaking.

He could see it, though. "Wassa matter? Gotta go?"

I nodded.

"Bad?"

I nodded faster.

His face was close.

His breath was deadly.

Max said, "Wassa matter, Nerd? Yo mamo feed you prunes for breakfast?"

Bubba looked at him over his shoulder. "It's ma*ma*, stupid."

Max shrank back. Then Bubba leaned his face

in even closer to mine, saying, "Did I hear you say you're gonna do my project for me?"

I shook my head.

"I *said*—" he grabbed me harder "—did I hear you say you're gonna do my project for me?"

I choked out, "No!" I tried to wrestle free. "Now let me go!"

He slugged me. Right in the stomach. I folded in two and fell on the floor, gasping for air.

My stomach was in a giant knot.

My chest caved in.

I felt like I was going to die.

Bubba stepped over me. Max and Kevin walked around me. All three of them were gone before I could move a muscle.

It took about five minutes for me to stand up. And when I did, I didn't run to a teacher to tell on Bubba. I locked myself in the stall and dug out my camera. Then I zoomed back through the movie clip and held my breath.

Had I caught him in the act? Had I recorded him flipping those trays? Did I get his face *and* the trays? My aim had been off so many times. Had I blown it again?

But all of a sudden I saw him on the monitor—mini-Bubba, looking over his shoulder at the teachers. Walking faster. Then *flip*, *flip*, *flip*, *flip*, *flip*, and he was gone.

I looked at the clip again.

And again.

I'd done it! I'd really done it!

Boy, was Bubba Bixby going to be sorry he'd ever laid a hand on Shredderman!

CHAPTER 8
Blastoff!

I downloaded the flip-o-rama clip, no problem. I linked it to my home page with a *The Bully in Action* button. Didn't even add words. The clip said it all.

Then I finished building a couple of other links I'd been working on: *Lullaby for Bubba* and *The Green Sheet Goblin*.

If you clicked on *Lullaby for Bubba*, you got a cheesy-sounding keyboard playing "Baa, Baa, Black Sheep" while my new words for the song scrolled over a background of Bubba's face:

Bubba bad sheep, throw him out of school
Yes sir, yes sir, he just breaks the rules
One, he's a liar

Two, he's a pain
Three, he's a bully
Bubba's got no shame.
Bubba bad sheep, throw him out of school
Yes sir, yes sir, he just breaks the rules

The Green Sheet Goblin linked to a page where a flying green ghost with Bubba's face went in a circle around:

Miriam Wipple!
Ian McCoy!
Danielle Duncan!
Your green sheets didn't just disappear,
The School Ghoul STOLE them!

Last but not least, I put in a site counter. That way I could tell how many people visited *shredderman.com.*

I checked all the pages over about twenty times, and when I was sure everything was perfect, I followed the steps for "going live." And then, with a final press of the Enter key, *shredder-*

man.com was launched into cyberspace.

My heart was beating really fast. And when the computer told me my site was now live, I sort of panicked. Had I really done it? Was *shredderman.com* really live?

I shut down my computer. I went to the bathroom and washed my face. It felt so hot. I looked at myself in the mirror for a long time. Was I Shredderman?

I went back to my room and booted up my computer. The address box appeared. My hands were shaking as I typed in *shredderman.com*.

I pressed Enter.

At the bottom of my screen I saw the blue connection line begin growing. Next to it flashed Web site found.

Then, Connecting. Waiting. Opening...

Then there he was, streaking across my screen—Shredderman!

"Wa-hoo!" I yelled. "Wa-hoo, wa-hoo, wa-hoo!"

A minute later there was a knock at my door. "Honey?"

I clicked off the monitor and tore open the door. "It works!"

"Your operation is a success?" my mom asked.

I gave her a bone-crushing hug. "Thank you! Thank you thank you thank you!"

"So *now* do we get to know what your project's about?"

I stepped back. "Uh...no!"

"Why not?"

"Uh...you can't! Not yet!"

She frowned at me. "Well, when?"

"I...I don't know."

We stared at each other.

Finally she said, "Nolan, I don't want you buried in your room alone all the time. And I don't like that you have secrets from me. You used to tell me everything!"

"I know, Mom. And I will! But not today."

"Hmmmm." She looked at me for the longest time. Finally she sighed and whispered, "You're really not going to let your dad help you with your project?"

I looked down.

"He really wanted to, you know."

I nodded, then kind of shrugged. "Parents aren't supposed to help."

"I know that, honey, but this is different. He

just wanted to be involved . . . not *do* it for you."

I kept looking down.

"I know your dad can get a little . . . *excited*. And you don't even have to take his suggestions. But isn't there something he can do to be part of this?"

I felt bad. Really bad. I'd been totally ignoring my dad. Actually, I'd been *avoiding* him, wishing I'd never said a word about the project.

But what was I supposed to do about it? If Dad knew I was doing my project on Bubba—not the mayor, or a policeman, or even his boss—he'd think I was being childish.

Vengeful.

Stupid.

So I just kept looking down and said, "I wanted it to be a . . . surprise."

"Oh," she said. And when I looked up, she was smiling.

Uh-oh. What did she think that meant? Did

she think I was doing something to surprise *them*?

She nodded and said, "I understand," then held my head and kissed me on the hair. And when she let go, she said, "Say, did you have a growth spurt?"

"Mo-om!"

"I used to have to stoop way over to smooch your head!"

"Mo-om!"

"I'm serious. And you *look* taller! In the morning I'm going to measure you."

I smiled back at her. My mom has a magic way of making me *feel* taller.

"Anyway. Do you know it's way past your bedtime? Again?"

I nodded. "I'm going."

"Good."

I double-brushed my teeth. Even wiped out the sink when I was done. But before I could actually go to sleep, I finished checking out the links on

my site. They worked great. The site looked great!
It was so, so cool!

I jumped into bed.

Closed my eyes.

And dreamed the best dreams ever.

Shredderman dreams.

CHAPTER 9
Spreading the Word

I got up early and checked the site again.

Still there!

And the site counter was at ... 2.

What good was a Web site if nobody knew about it? And how could I tell anyone about it without giving away that I'd built the site?

They'd know right off that I was Shredderman!

Maybe I could get e-mail addresses from the kids in my class and Shredderman could send them the link!

Nah. Getting the addresses would take too long. Plus, it'd be really obvious.

Maybe I could tape flyers up around school before the teachers got there!

Nah. Mr. Hoover would take them down by the time they let kids on campus.

So how was I going to spread the word? There had to be some way to do it before the teachers could stop me.

But how? How could I let kids know about the Shredderman site without giving myself away?

I looked out my window over at the school and saw the American flag being hoisted up the pole. Boy, Mr. Hoover started working early! I wouldn't be able to do anything with him around!

I watched the flag flutter in the breeze, and that's when I got the idea.

Confetti.

Mr. Hoover was always picking up trash. He couldn't keep up! What if there were pieces of paper all over the playgrounds? Colored paper! Kids would *have* to notice them! And Mr. Hoover and all the teachers put together couldn't pick them all up—they'd make the kids do it!

Oh, yeah!

I got to work making confetti. Big confetti. Lots of confetti. I made a document on my computer that had a bunch of different things on it. Like:

Does Bubba Bixby cause you grief? Try

SHREDDERMAN.COM

for comic relief.

*

Hey Bubba!

Get yo mama to go to

SHREDDERMAN.COM!

*

SHREDDERMAN.COM

Where the good guys shred!

*

POW! KA-BAM! SMACK!

Shredderman KO's Bubba for you on

SHREDDERMAN.COM

Next, I copied and pasted as many as would fit

on one page, put purple paper in the printer, and let her rip!

I got ready for school!

I gobbled down breakfast!

And when I was out of purple paper, I put in yellow.

My printer was flying!

And while it was printing, I cut the finished papers into strips. Hundreds and hundreds of strips! By the time the school bells were ringing, I had a couple of gallon-sized Ziplocs filled with super-sized confetti and I was ready to use it!

But how?

I couldn't let anyone see me throw it around. They'd know I was Shredderman.

I'd have to be sly.

Quick.

Smart.

I double-checked my shoelaces. This was no time to trip up!

"Are you all right, honey?" my mom asked as I was heading out the door.

"Yeah, great!" I told her.

She felt my forehead anyway. "You look flushed."

"I'm fine," I said.

She smiled. "Hey! I forgot to measure you. You've got time, come here."

"No, Mom! I've already got my shoes on! It's not like I'm going to shrink or anything. I've got to get to school!"

"Okay, tomorrow then." She grabbed my head

and kissed it and called, "Nice job on your hair!" as I beat it out the door.

Brother. Superheroes don't get kissed on the top of their head!

I did my power-walk and got to school fast. And the same two kids who said, "Slow down, Nerd!" before were hanging out on the steps and they said it again.

I was two power steps past them when all of a sudden I stopped, turned around, and went back.

Their eyes opened a little in surprise.

"Hi," I said. "My name's Nolan. What's yours?"

"Uh, Eddie."

"Uh...Matt."

"Hi, Eddie. Hi, Matt. Please don't call me Nerd anymore, okay? My name's Nolan."

Eddie laughed. "But, dude, you do that funky walk. It looks so geeky."

"But it's fast!" I said. "Don't you ever have to get somewhere fast when you're not supposed to run?"

They both shrugged.

Then Matt said, "But no way I'd walk like *that*."

"Well, it may look funny, but it works great. Anyway, call me Nolan, okay?"

"Sure," they both said.

I blinked. Wow. They said "Sure." No "Nerd" added at the last second, just "Sure." I smiled at them and took off.

I might have been able to throw a few handfuls of confetti around before we had to go to class, but there were two reasons why I didn't: One, I didn't want just a few papers here and there— I wanted papers everywhere! And two, I couldn't risk anyone seeing me.

Anyone.

I looked around at all the kids. At all the classroom windows. How was I ever going to get my confetti everywhere without being seen?

The breeze was still blowing. If only I could get my confetti into the wind! If only I could get it to sail across the playground and scatter everywhere!

But how?

I looked up. If I could get on the roof of a portable classroom, the breeze would carry my confetti much farther than if I just scattered it at ground level.

I checked the direction that the breeze was

blowing. If I wanted the confetti to blow across the playground, I'd have to climb onto Room 17 or 18, or the computer lab.

But how was I going to get on the roof? The portables all had ramp rails and downspouts, but I'd never make it. It was too straight up.

I ran behind the portables. Same story. But Mr. Hoover's pickup truck was parked behind the computer lab....

I moved closer.

I could climb on Mr. Hoover's truck and then ... there was a power panel box on the computer lab wall! Plus a pipe coming out of the power panel and going up. And then there was the backside of the air conditioner ... and a big floodlight, too! If I could get up to the air conditioner, I could get on the roof!

Or at least, Shredderman could.

The last bell rang, so I ran to class. Was I really going to do this? Could I really climb a roof? I had trouble climbing little trees and monkey bars. A *roof*?

I couldn't pay attention in class. All I could think about was, could I do it? Would Mr. Hoover move his truck before I could try? What if I fell and no one found me?

What if I got caught?

Then, in the middle of watching a scorpion battle a rat on a nature video, I put up the signal for having to use the bathroom.

Mr. Green saw me and gave me the nod.

I snuck through the dark with my backpack, and out the door.

I looked all around.

The coast was clear.

It was time for Shredderman to climb a roof!

CHAPTER 10
Confetti Hits the Fan

Mr. Hoover's truck was still there.

Wa-hoo!

I strapped on my pack, jumped in the back, and climbed on the cab roof. The metal buckled a little under my feet.

Oops.

I lifted one foot onto the computer lab's power panel.

I grabbed the pipe.

I pulled myself up!

Then I just stood there, flat against the wall. If the truck wasn't there, I'd be in trouble. It was a long way down!

Okay, I told myself, get moving.

I reached for the air conditioner with one hand and held on to the pipe with the other. It was farther away than it looked from the ground. Higher up, too.

Don't look down, I told myself. Don't look down.

I glued my eyes to the air conditioner. My right hand had a good grip over the top of it, and I was about to go for it when I felt something tickling my hand.

It was creepy.

Crawly.

And the next thing I knew, a big black spider was dive-bombing me from the air conditioner.

"Aaarrgh!"

I swatted, I shook. I panicked, I slipped. And when it was all over, the spider had disappeared and I was hanging on to the pipe, scared out of my mind.

One toe was wedged onto one of the brackets

that held the pipe to the wall. The other foot was dangling around looking for something to grip on to.

I tried to reach the air conditioner, but I couldn't.

I couldn't go back to the power panel, either.

Could I pull myself up the pipe? Maybe if I got higher, I could get my foot on the air conditioner.

Inch by inch, I pulled myself up, wishing I could climb walls like The Gecko. I used muscles I didn't even know were there. I grabbed toe-holds that didn't even look as big as a toe. I cut my hand on a bracket. I learned what sweating bullets means.

But I did it. I got myself onto the air conditioner.

I stood on it for a minute, catching my breath. Shaking.

Shredderman was definitely not The Gecko. Or Spider-Man.

But there I was. My head was above the roof. All I had to do was get the rest of me up there.

I reached up, swung my foot to the floodlight, pushed off, and pulled up.

Two seconds later, Shredderman was on the roof. Wa-hoo!

I hunched over and tiptoed across the middle of the roof, trying not to make any noise. It seemed like such a long way from the back to the front!

When I was almost there, I dropped down on all fours and crawled. At the edge, I peeked over.

A kid was going into Room 20.

The door closed.

I looked left.

I looked right.

No one else was around!

I peeled off my backpack and dug out the Ziploc bags. I started flinging handfuls of confetti into the air. Whoosh! Whoosh! Whoosh!

I went into speedy mode and scattered the rest of the first bag.

I shook out the second bag!

Purple and yellow paper fluttered up, down, out . . . it was flying everywhere!

It was beautiful!

Awesome!

Amazing!

I felt like throwing both my arms in the air and shouting, "Shredderman lives!" Instead, I grabbed my stuff and ran across the roof, back to the air conditioner.

And when I looked down, Mr. Hoover's truck was pulling away.

Uh-*oh*.

I stood there a minute, not knowing what to do. Superheroes don't call for help. They *are* the help. And I had to get down from there *fast*.

So I took a deep breath and lowered myself over the roof and onto the air conditioner.

I sat down on the air conditioner and reached for the pipe, telling myself, You can do this. You *can* do this.

I grabbed the pipe with one hand, held on to the air conditioner with the other, then let myself down, with one foot pushing against the side of the air conditioner, the other against the pipe.

When I got a toehold on a pipe bracket, I pushed off of the air conditioner, hung on the pipe for a second, then swung over to the power panel.

So far, down was much easier than up.

And if the truck had still been there, it would have been all over. But the truck was gone and now I only had one choice.

Jump.

One, two, three! I pushed off and flew to the ground.

Guess what. Shredderman is not Superman, either. I landed hard, fell over, and scraped both hands and an arm.

Everything hurt, but nothing was broken. So after a few seconds of shaking off the pain, I got up and dusted off. Then I snuck around the building and back to class.

The video was still going, so I squeezed through the door and slid into my seat.

Mr. Green was talking with a student over in the corner. The kids at my table were watching a snake swallow something with a really long tail. No one even seemed to notice I'd been gone.

Mission impossible, not so impossible!

And as I sat there catching my breath, I couldn't stop thinking about what I'd just done. How being Shredderman was making me *do* things that I'd only ever dreamed about before.

Maybe I was banged up and scraped up, but I felt good.

No, I felt great!

And for once I had something in common with every other kid at school—I couldn't wait for recess.

CHAPTER 11
Dr. Voss Comes Knocking

When the recess bell finally rang, I waited until almost everyone else was out the door. And when I did go outside, all my beautiful, awesome papers were just lying there.

Like trash.

Kids were walking on them. Running over them.

Ignoring them.

I felt like calling, Hey! Check out the confetti. *Read* it! Instead, I walked around with a lump in my throat.

Then I heard one of the fourth-grade teachers say, "What in the world? Look at this mess!" She picked up a purple slip and read it.

She picked up another.

And another.

Pretty soon she had a whole handful of confetti.

A girl came up to her and said, "What *is* that, Mrs. Bernhart?" and picked one up, too.

Mrs. Bernhart blinked around at the blacktop and sand. Her mouth was hanging open. She ripped the paper out of the girl's hand. Then *she* did a power-walk. Straight for the office.

The girl picked another strip off the ground and read it. "Hey!" she called to a friend. "Look at this!"

That's all it took. It spread like a cyber-virus around the playground. Everyone was picking up slips. Everyone was talking to their friends. Kids were smiling. Laughing. Giggling. Showing each other what their slip said. And they were running all over the place to see if there was more. Something on a slip they hadn't read yet. There wasn't a ball bouncing anywhere on the playground!

I could hear their voices. "Shredderman...? Shredderman...Shredderman...!" It was quiet at first, but got louder. And louder! Like a swarm of bees getting bigger and bigger.

Mrs. Bernhart came back, and she wasn't alone. Another teacher, Miss Simms, was with her. So was our principal, Dr. Voss!

Pretty soon *all* the teachers were in a huddle near the bathrooms. Even Mr. Green. They were talking rapid-fire, too. Hands were waving. Heads were shaking. They didn't know what to do. It was too late to stop it.

Then Freddy came up from behind me and shoved my shoulder. "Why are you just standing here, Nerd?"

I caught my balance, then turned and shoved him back.

Hard.

And before I could believe I'd done that, out of my mouth popped, "Nothing, okay, *Pee-boy?*"

He blinked at me, then just stood there like I'd hit him with a stun gun.

I took a step back and said, "You're Freddy, I'm Nolan. Got it?"

He nodded.

Then he followed me as I walked away, saying, "I just couldn't believe you weren't checking these out." He handed me a purple slip. "They're about Bubba."

"Bubba?" I said, trying to act like I didn't know anything about it. "What's this Shredderman stuff about?"

"I don't know! But I sure want to check it out. You think Miss Surkit will let us on the Internet?"

I blinked at him. And I wanted to say, Us? but instead I laughed and said, "Worth a try!"

The computer lab was open, but we didn't see Miss Surkit right away. She's really short—even shorter than most of the upper graders—so it's easy to miss her. But Freddy spotted her behind her computer.

"Miss Surkit?" I asked. She was grinning from ear to ear.

"Huh?" she said, looking up.

Before she could switch back to the browser's home page, I saw *my* home page flash on her monitor.

She'd been visiting *shredderman.com*!

"Yes, Nolan? Well, hi there, Freddy."

I said, "We were wondering if we could use the Internet?"

She raised an eyebrow and asked, "Was there a particular *site* you wanted to visit?" She picked a piece of confetti off her desk and wagged it at us. "I don't think Dr. Voss is going to permit visits to *shredderman.com*, if that's what you're after."

"Darn!" Freddy said.

"Bummer," I added, trying hard not to smile.

As we left the computer lab, Freddy said, "Wow. If they're censoring it, it must be *good*."

Then he took off down the ramp, calling, "See you back in class."

By the end of recess, confetti was in pockets everywhere. There was almost none of it left on the ground.

Back in class, people tried to ask Bubba what was going on, but he just got mad. "I don't know, stupid! You think I know? How am I supposed to know, huh?"

Then, like a couple of dumbmunks, Kevin and Max said, "Yeah, how's he supposed to know, huh?"

Mr. Green had barely gotten everyone to quit talking when Dr. Voss came into the room.

My heart stopped.

I could see it on her face—she knew!

Boy, was I in deep, deep doo-doo.

Dr. Voss whispered something to Mr. Green.

They both looked very serious.

Then Dr. Voss left the room, but we could see her waiting outside.

Mr. Green said, "Okay, gang. Take out your social studies books and begin reading on page one-forty-nine. We'll be answering questions at the end of the section. Numbers one through ten."

We pulled out our books.

We turned to page 149.

We looked at Dr. Voss, waiting outside.

Then Mr. Green moved between the tables. He was headed straight for ours! My heart was pounding. How had they figured it out? How had I given myself away? I'd even registered *shredderman.com* to Shredderman. I hadn't used any part of my real name anywhere!

But Mr. Green didn't stop at our table. He walked right past me.

Right over to Table 6.

And two seconds later, it was Bubba Bixby, not me, who was on his way to the office.

CHAPTER 12

Yours in Truth and Justice

I didn't see Bubba again for the rest of the day. But at lunch, kids in the food line were all talking about him.

"Where's Bubba?"

"Someone said he was hauled off by Dr. Voss!"

"What did he do?"

"I don't know...but he must've done something wickeder than usual."

"I can't wait to check out that Shredderman site."

"Me neither."

I kept my head down and my mouth shut. At the lunch tables, no one knew anything, either, but everyone was guessing.

"I bet Bubba got suspended."

"Maybe expelled!"

"It's about time."

"No kidding!"

"What if *he's* Shredderman?"

"Can't be. Didn't you *read* these?"

"Yeah, but . . . what's 'comic' mean, anyway?"

"Funny, stupid. Like comedian?"

"Don't call me stupid, or I'll call you Bubba."

"Oh, sorry."

I just drank my milk and tried to keep a stra
face.

It was actually pretty quiet for the rest
day. Mr. Green seemed really spacey. He ev
got our fifteen minutes of music time,
never forgets music time.

After school, I charged home. I didn'
power-walk, either. I ran!

"Have a good day, honey?" my mom a
her computer.

"Great!" I said, and peeled off my backpack. "The best!"

"Really? What happened?" Then she noticed my arm. "Hey...that's quite a scrape."

"Yeah, I...I fell down."

"Oooh, your hands, too," she said, flipping them over. "Let's clean them up, huh?"

Do superheroes let their moms clean them with iodine? I doubt it, but there was no getting out of it. And while I cringed and hissed, she said, "So, tell me—what was so great about today?"

"I...well, I stuck up for myself. Twice."

"Oh?" One of her eyebrows reached for the sky.

"Yeah. Once when these two older guys were making fun of my power-walk, and once when Freddy called me Nerd."

"Really?" she said. "That's wonderful news! Good for you!"

"It worked out fine, too. I think those sixth

106

graders might actually try my power-walk some-time." Then I added, "It gets you places fast."

Her eyes twinkled. "I know."

She rubbed me down with Neosporin, then kissed me on the head and said, "I'm proud of you for sticking up for yourself, honey."

"Thanks, Mom."

She cut me some apples and cheese, and after I'd wolfed those down, I went straight to my room.

I booted up, loaded *shredderman.com*, and scrolled straight to the site counter.

It said 27.

Already?

Oh, yeah!

And there were e-mail messages for shredder-man@shredderman.com! Seven of them!

I read them all quick. Six were good, one was bad—said they thought *Alvin and the Dumb-munks* was the stupidest thing they'd ever seen.

Probably sent by Kevin or Max.

But the good ones were great! Someone said: *Shredderman, you rock! Keep on shredding!*

Someone else said: *How'd you catch him? I can't believe it! Who ARE you????? P.S. Can I be your side-kick?*

I answered every one and signed them all: *Yours in truth and justice, Shredderman.*

It was more fun than Christmas.

Then I copied the messages that didn't have bad words and pasted them into a new *This Just In* link, leaving the person's name off if they'd signed it.

I wanted to just sit there, refreshing the site, waiting for the counter to go up or more e-mails to come in, but I made myself shut down. Then I kept on shredding, right through my homework. When Mom called, "Dinner!" I raced to the table. I was starving! I ate lasagna! Beans! Salad! More lasagna! More beans! More salad!

Being a superhero sure gives you an appetite.

My father said, "You having a growth spurt, champ?"

My mother said, "See, Nolan?"

I said, "What's for dessert?"

After I cleared the dishes, I ditched it back to my room. Computer on . . . site loaded . . . *shredderman.com* was up to . . . seventy-three hits!

Wa-*hoo*!

There was more e-mail, too.

I scrolled through them, but froze about halfway down. There was a message from bixby@bignet.com.

Uh-oh.

I opened the file, hoping my virus protection was working. The message was from Bubba, all right. And it said:

I know who you are you ugly turd. You're gonna be sorry you were ever born!

Uh-triple-*oh*!

I sat there for a long time, looking at it. Could he really have found out it was me? What would he do to me if he *did* know?

Pound me?

Crush me?

Kill me?

But wouldn't he have put "you stupid nerd" instead of "you ugly turd" if he knew it was me?

I answered the rest of the e-mails, then finally hit the Reply button on Bubba's message. And after staring at the screen for a minute, I typed:

Alvin:

You're right—you do know me. I'm everyone you've ever beaten up or threatened. Everyone you've ever made fun of or robbed. You see me, all right. Every time you turn around. So look out. I'm watching.

Yours in truth and justice,

Shredderman

I pressed Send, and added the conversation to the *This Just In* page. Then I shut down and got ready for bed early.

It was dangerous being a superhero.

A little scary, too.

What if Bubba really did know?

Tomorrow, I'd find out.

CHAPTER 13
Miracle at Table 4

The next day, the buzz was even louder. Everyone was talking about *shredderman.com*. Even the teachers.

I'd left my camera at home, and Bubba didn't seem to be around anywhere, so I played four-square like I used to. The kids in line were all saying how they'd visited the site, or heard about the site, or were *going* to visit the site.

Some kids in front of me—who usually ignore me or call me Nerd—even asked me if I'd seen it. I smiled and said, "What do you call a bully fire?"

"A Bubba-que!" they cried, and we all laughed.

When it was my turn to play, Ronnie Stalwess

was server. He said, "Easy out!" like all the kids always do when I get in.

I backed up.

I dug in.

Not this time, I told myself. Not this time.

He served me the ball.

I hit it to square three.

It came slamming back.

I slapped it to Ronnie.

Ronnie shot it straight at me.

I jumped to the side. The ball was out!

Ronnie said, "Maaan!" and went to the end of the line.

When the last bell rang, I was standing in square two. Square two! One of these days, I'd make it to server.

One of these days, *I'd* call the rules.

Yes, I would!

I ran to class along with everyone else. We said the pledge. Mr. Green called for absences.

Jenni said, "Bubba!" Everyone looked.

No Bubba.

I'd already noticed that. It was the first thing I'd looked for when I'd sat in my seat.

"Okay, gang," Mr. Green said from his desk, "before we begin, Miriam, Ian, Danielle...," he waved three green sheets in the air, "...I have something for you."

They ran up, saying, "Thank you, Mr. Green! Thank you!"

"Thank Shredderman," he said with a grin. "He's the one who shed light on the situation." He nodded over at Table 1. "What is it, Kayla?" Her hand was flapping in the air.

"Some people are saying that *you're* Shredderman. Is that true?"

"*Me?*" Mr. Green asked, then laughed. "Where did you hear that?"

"From some kids on the playground. Sixth graders."

"Well," Mr. Green said. Then he grinned and added, "Dr. Voss accused me of the same thing."

"Well?" Kayla asked. "Are you?"

His mouth went left, right, all around. He grabbed his guitar and strummed it. Faster. Then faster. And faster! His hand was just a *blur*.

When he stopped, Kayla said, "I'll take that as a yes?"

"Don't," he said. "Take it as an, I'm not telling."

"But, Mr. Green...!"

"I think Shredderman put it best— he is all of us."

"But, Mr. Green...!"

"Yeah, Mr. Green, tell us!" everyone else was saying. "We can keep a secret."

"Oh, right," he said with a grin.

"Really!" Kayla said. "We can!"

"Well, gang, the truth is..." He looked around the classroom. Everyone held their breath. "That Web site is not mine."

"It's *not?*"

He shook his head.

"So whose is it? And where's Bubba?"

"Let's all call him Alvin, shall we?"

Brian said, "That's too weird, Mr. Green."

Ian added, "Yeah. It's also dangerous."

"Not if you *all* call him Alvin," Mr. Green said. "Calling him Bubba just feeds into that whole...*image* he's trying to build for himself. Don't enable him. Just call him Alvin." Then he added, "Alvin and his parents are meeting with Dr. Voss today. He'll probably be out all day."

"But did you see that e-mail? He said he knows who Shredderman is! Do you think he does?"

Mr. Green noodled a little on his guitar, then said, "No." He looked around the classroom. "Do you?"

People shook their heads.

"Which brings us back to what Shredderman said to Alvin in his message. He—or *she*—is everyone."

"She?"

"Well, sure. What if it's a girl—or woman—who's trying to throw you off track?"

Everyone started whispering.

Mr. Green laughed.

"What I think you should do is imagine that Shredderman is the person next to you. And imagine that they can put the things you say and do on the Shredderman Web site." He leaned across his guitar. "How are you going to act? Snotty? Some of you can get wicked snotty.

Nasty? You think I can't hear you dogging each other? C'mon!" He smiled and said, "The beauty of Shredderman is that you *don't* know who it is. He or she could be anybody!" He leaned back, strummed a few chords, then said, "It's what you do when you think no one's looking that tells us what kind of person you really are. And maybe if you thought that someone was always watching you, you'd get in the habit of being a little nicer to each other."

No one said a word.

"So," he said with a final strum, "pretend Shredderman's the person standing next to you, sitting next to you, walking next to you... then act accordingly."

All the tables looked around at each other.

Everyone was wondering, Are *you* Shredderman?

Randy blinked at me.

I kept a straight face and blinked back.

Freddy looked at Randy, then at me.

Trinity looked around, too, then smiled at me.

I smiled back. And I kept on smiling, too. First at Freddy, then at Randy.

Then a miracle happened at Table 4.

Both of them smiled back at me.

CHAPTER 14
Shredderman Gets a Sidekick

It was lunchtime. Everyone was charging the door, me included. I hate getting to the lunch line late. You waste too much lunch recess waiting. I wanted to play four-square. Maybe I'd make server!

But Mr. Green stopped me. "Nolan!" he called. "Come here a sec."

I went to his desk, where he was stacking the science papers we'd just turned in. "Yes, Mr. Green?"

"How's your project coming along?"

"Uh...fine."

"Having any problems with it?"

I shook my head.

The classroom was empty now, except for him and me. "What are you doing it on?" he asked.

Uh-oh.

"Nolan?"

"Yes, sir?"

"What's the subject?"

"Uh, well, actually, I keep starting over."

His eyebrows went up.

He sat down.

"Oh, really?"

"Yeah." I started talking really fast. "My dad wanted me to do it on the mayor, but I didn't want to. So he said to do it on his *boss*, but his boss makes him work too much and he's kind of *mean* to him. So then he said I should do it on Sarge—"

"Sarge?"

"He's a friend of my dad's. He's on the police force."

"Ah."

"So I've been um … I've been working on …" I didn't want to lie to him! What was I going to say?

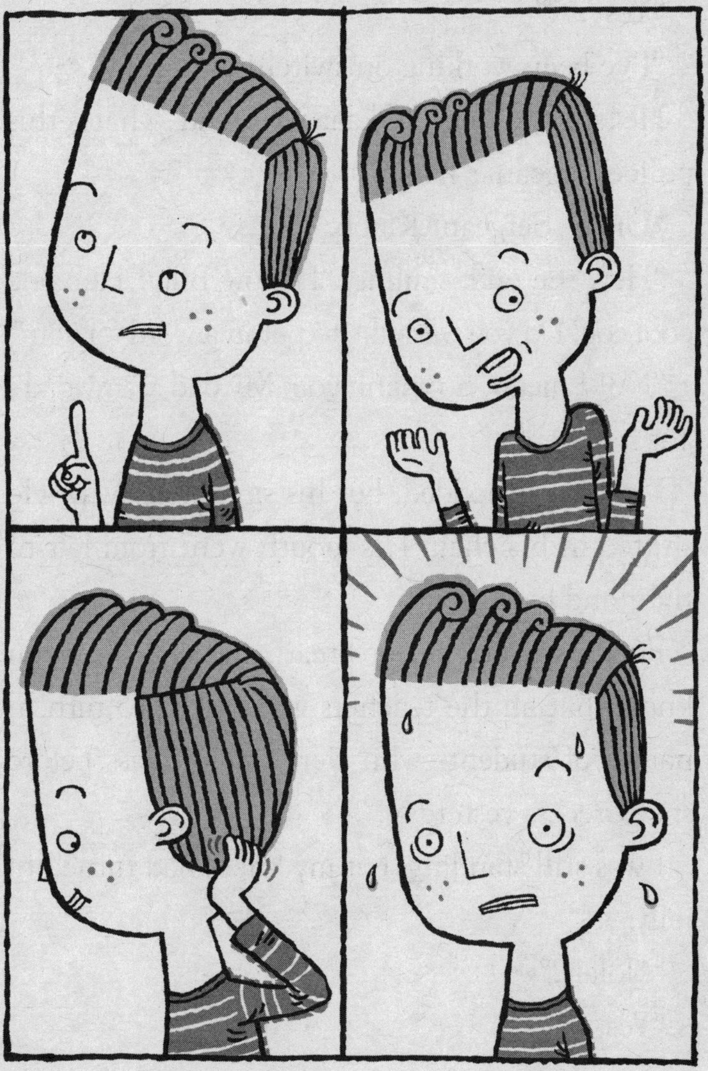

"Yes...?"

"I've been working on switching to him."

He studied me. "Okaaaaay. And what's this police sergeant's name?"

"Um...Sergeant Klubb."

"Hey," he said, smiling, "I know Billy! He's one cool cop. Do you want me to put in a word for you?"

"No! I mean, no thank you. My dad...my dad's got it covered."

Mr. Green nodded, but his smile fell away. He shifted in his chair. His mouth went from left to right and back again.

Finally he took a deep breath and said, "Did you know that all the teachers were asked to turn in names of students who were out of class before snack recess yesterday?"

I was still standing, but my knees had turned to jelly.

"Nolan?"

"Yes, sir?"

"Did you hear me?"

"Yes, sir."

"Are you worried?"

"Worried?" I was sweating cannonballs!

"That I turned in your name."

I shook my head.

"Really." He cocked his head. "I thought you might be."

I shrugged. "Why?"

He leaned back, his hands folded behind his head. A foot kicked onto the science papers. The other came up and crossed it. Finally he said, "You're being very cool about this, Shredderman."

Uh-quadruple-oh! "Me?" I said.

"Have a seat, Nolan."

I sat.

"It's okay, Nolan. I didn't turn your name in."

"You didn't? I mean, you could have…."

He put up a hand. "I have an apology to make, so please hear me out."

I nodded.

"Earlier in the year you tried to tell me things about Alvin. It's clear that I didn't take them seriously enough. But I want you to know that from now on, if you have a problem with someone, I'll listen better. There's a lot going on in class, but that's no reason for things to have come to this point. I should have paid more attention, and I'm sorry."

I started to tell him that it wasn't *his* fault Bubba was born big and mean, full of teeth and ready to bite, but he put up his hand again and said, "The situation with Alvin is pretty complex, but again, that's no excuse. And off the record? Your solution is brilliant. Very well executed, I might add." He shook his head and chuckled. "All this time I thought you were shy, but you're a real comedian, you know that? I laughed my head off."

I hadn't admitted anything yet. And even

though I wanted to tell him he was right—that I *had* built the site—it felt like it would be the end of Shredderman if I did. "But, Mr. Green, I'm not Shredderman."

His feet swung off the desk.

He leaned forward.

Then he whispered, "I'm not going to breathe a word of this to anyone, Nolan. You cover your tracks by turning in a real project, and I'll make sure no one suspects it's you."

I just stood there, staring at him.

"Look. I love Shredderman! I think what you've done is going to change the tone of this campus. Let me help you! Your site could be so much more than All Bubba, All the Time. Think about what you can do with it! You could post kids doing *nice* things to each other! Have mystery guests. Or riddles about kids no one knows very well. There's a ton you can do with your site. Good stuff!"

"But—"

"Come on," he laughed. "Superman had Jimmy Olsen! Batman had Robin! Shoot, even The Gecko's got Sticky, right? Shredderman needs an ally." He leaned in a little closer. "Nolan, let me be your sidekick."

A teacher as a sidekick?

I laughed out loud. And I was about to say, Really? but he stopped me. "You don't have to say a word," he whispered, then put out his hand.

I looked at him a minute, then shook it.

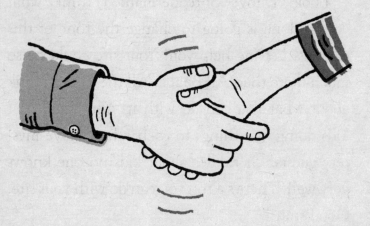

CHAPTER 15
Mr. Bixby

After lunch, it was like my conversation with Mr. Green had never happened. He taught, he sang, he read a story. He was just Mr. Green.

He sure wasn't *acting* like a sidekick!

And after school, he stood at the door and said bye to us like he usually does. "Don't forget your lunchbox, Sarah.... Good luck at your game this afternoon, Andrew.... Hey, Danielle, your backpack's wide open.... See ya, Myles.... Keep smiling, Trinity...." When I came past, he said, "Stay cool, dude," and gave me a wink.

I didn't go straight home. I sat on a bench at the edge of the playground, thinking. What was I going to do with my Web site now?

And what was happening to Bubba, anyway? Were they going to make him be nicer?

Could they do that?

Were they going to kick him out of school?

And if they did, why have a Web site?

Why be Shredderman?

Mr. Green seemed to think there was lots more I could do with the site, but right then I was thinking that maybe I should just tear it down.

Then I spotted Bubba. He was out in the parking lot, standing between his mother and father.

I jumped off the bench and moved closer.

I hid behind a tree and watched.

Bubba's dad was unlocking their car and yelling at Mrs. Bixby.

Mrs. Bixby started yelling back, but he grabbed her by the arm and kind of shoved her into the car.

Then Mr. Bixby started yelling at Bubba, and when Bubba said something back, Mr. Bixby

popped him across his head and shouted, "I said, get inside!"

Where was my camera? Boy! That Mr. Bixby was big and mean. A real bully!

All of a sudden I was Shredderman again, only this time I wanted to *defend* Bubba. How could his father be so mean?

There was nothing I could do, though. Not now anyway. They were already driving away.

And as I watched their car peel out of the parking lot, I thought that maybe Bubba Bixby *wasn't* born big and mean, full of teeth and ready to bite.

Maybe Bubba had learned it from his dad.

I wandered home, thinking about Bubba's dad. About my dad. What a difference!

And it made me think about how lucky I was— my dad had never treated me like that.

Ever.

By the time I got home, I had a new plan. A

cool plan! One I couldn't wait to get started on!

"Mom!" I shouted when I burst through the door.

"In here!" she called from the kitchen.

"Hey! Can you take me over to the *Gazette*?"

"The *Gazette*? Why?"

"I want to see Dad. Right away."

She stopped smearing peanut butter in a celery stick. "Is everything all right?"

I took the celery stick. "Everything's great!" I chomped through peanut butter and said, "I want to talk to him about my project!"

"You do?"

"Uh-huh! Can we go?"

She dropped everything, grabbed her purse, and off we went. And when we got to Dad's cubicle at the *Gazette*, Mom leaned around the corner and said, "Surprise!"

"Eve!" Dad said, standing up. Then he noticed me. "Nolan!"

"Hi, Dad!"

"Hey! I'm glad you caught me. I actually just got in from an assignment. Mr. Zilch had me chasing down some—"

"Steven," my mom laughed, "don't you want to know why we're here?"

"Of course!" He looked at me. "You look like you have big news."

I shrugged. "Well, no. I just changed my mind."

"About your...?" I could tell he was hoping it was about my project but didn't want to risk guessing.

I nodded. "About my project."

"Well!" he said, a smile stretching across his face. He glanced at my mom, but she shook her head and said, "I had nothing to do with this, Steven, I promise. He came home from school wanting to see you."

"So!" my dad said, smiling at me. "Am I calling the mayor? Mr. Zilch? Sarge?"

I shook my head. "I want to do my project on someone better than them."

"Shhh!" Dad whispered, looking around for Mr. Zilch. "Uh, who do you have in mind?"

"Someone better than the mayor, or any sports hero, or the president, or even Bill Gates!"

"Someone better than . . . ?" His voice trailed off and he took a deep breath. "Nolan, when I said I could get you in touch with people, I meant in this community. I didn't mean the president. Or Bill Gates!"

"Da-ad!" I said, grinning. "Someone *better* than them!"

His eyes shifted from me to my mom and back again.

I laughed. "I want to do my project on you!"

He stared at me.

He stared some more.

Then his chin started quivering.

"On . . . *me* . . . ?"

I nodded.

He gave me a hug. Even picked me off the floor
a little!

"Da-ad!" I said, but it felt good.

Super good.

CHAPTER 16
Shredderman Lives!

When Bubba came back to school, he was meaner than ever.

He called us names.

He shoved.

He yelled.

He hadn't changed a bit.

What *had* changed was everyone else.

"My name's not Stupid, Alvin, it's Rodney."

"Hey, Alvin! The back of the line's over there! Quit trying to cut."

"No, I'm not gonna give you money. Ask yo mama to give you dough!"

Even Max and Kevin were avoiding him. "You think I want to be a dumbmunk the rest of my life? No way!"

Things *had* changed.

Things *were* better.

For me, too.

For one thing, I got my name back. Only two people called me Nerd all day, and believe me, I set them straight.

For another, I *feel* different.

Stronger.

Smarter.

Braver.

Like a superhero should.

And maybe I can't leap tall buildings in a single bound. Or stop a locomotive from steaming down the track. Maybe I can't even make it to server on the four-square court. But inside, I'm happy.

Inside, I know I *can* find ways to fight for truth and justice.

Inside, I know I *can* change the world—even if it's just my little corner of it.

Inside, Shredderman lives!